USHA and the BIG DIGGER

Amitha Jagannath Knight

Illustrated by **Sandhya Prabhat**

ini **Charlesbridge**

Usha loved trucks.
She made them bump and roll.

Usha loved cartwheels too.
If only she could do one!

Flippety

thump.

Flippety

thump.

CRASH!

"Watch out!" said her big sister, Aarti.

"Sorry," said Usha. "Can you teach me to cartwheel?"

"I'm busy," said Aarti. "I just found the Big Dipper."

"What's a dipper?" asked Usha. "Show me!"

"It's a big spoon," said Aarti. "See that box of four stars? Connect the dots to make the scoop. The other three stars make the handle."

"Ooh! I see the scoop!" shouted Usha. "Look out, stars . . .

"It's the Big **DIGGER!**
That tree on the right points
to the driver. Beep beep!"

"No way," said Aarti. "The tree is on the left. It points to the dipper's handle. Can't you tell your left from your right?"

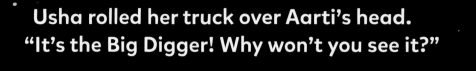

Usha rolled her truck over Aarti's head.
"It's the Big Digger! Why won't you see it?"

"Quit it!" snapped Aarti. "It's the
Big Dipper! Everyone says so."

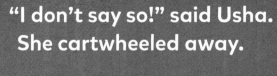

"I don't say so!" said Usha.
She cartwheeled away.

Flippety thump.

Flippety thump.

Flippety thump—

SPLAT!

The next night, their cousin Gloria arrived.

She gave Usha a brand-new truck.

"Thanks!" Usha said. "Now come outside.
I'll show you an even **BIGGER** truck!"

The girls looked up. "See, Gloria? It's the Big Digger," said Usha.

"It's still the Big Dipper," Aarti grumbled.

"Hmm . . ." said Gloria. "I see . . .

"the Big Kite!"

"What?" cried Usha and Aarti.

"The top four stars are the kite, and the bottom three stars are the tail," said Gloria.

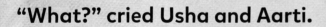
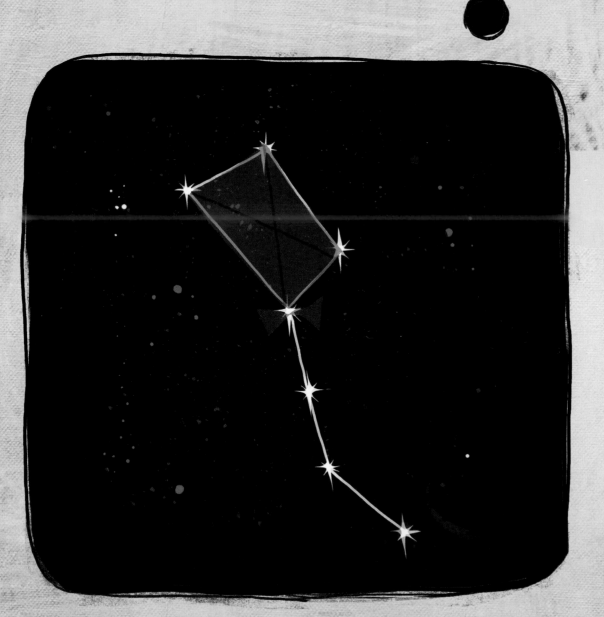

"Why can't anyone see my Big Digger?" Usha moaned.

"Because it's really the Big Dipper," Aarti groaned.

"Don't you like my kite?" asked Gloria.

"It's too loud over here," Aarti said. "Come on, Gloria!"

Whirly swirl! *Whirly swirl!* *Whirly swirly whooosh!*

Usha got mad.

Usha got sad.

She wanted to cartwheel too!

Flippety

thump—

Usha looked up.

Was that . . . the Big Dipper?
What about her truck?

**"Big Digger, where
are you?"**

OOF!

She tried more cartwheels.

Flippety thump.

She saw the Big Kite.

Flippety thump.

There were all kinds of shapes in the stars.

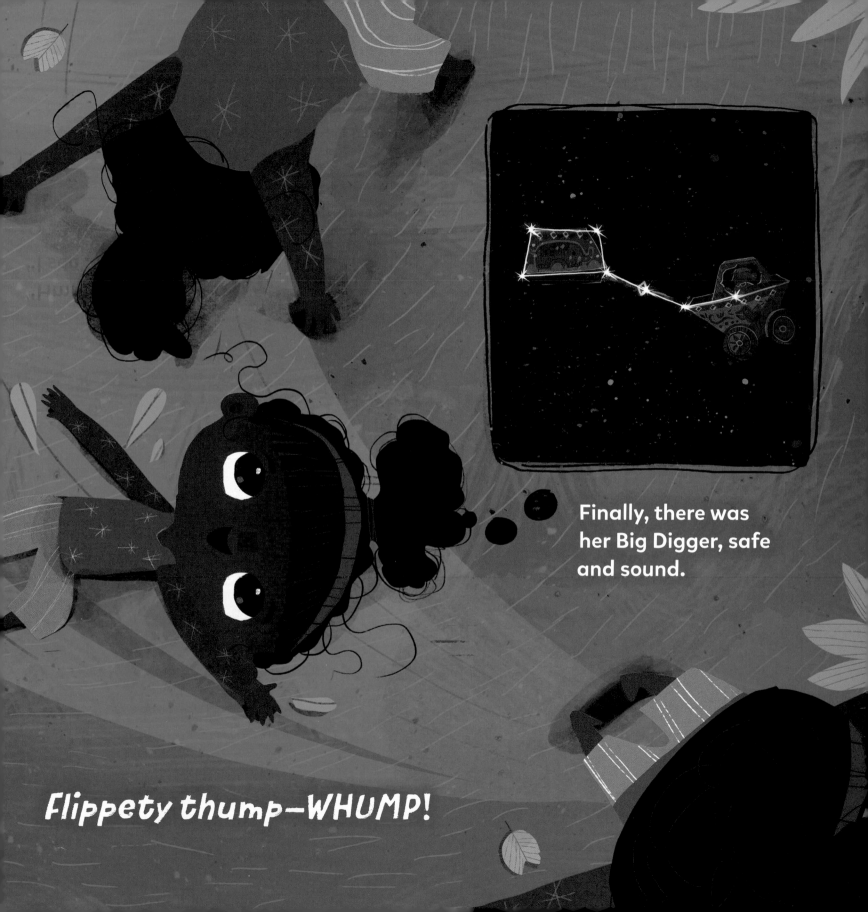

Finally, there was her Big Digger, safe and sound.

Flippety thump–WHUMP!

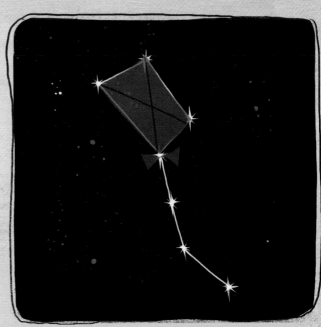

"Aarti! Gloria! Come back!" called Usha. "Lie here and look up."

"It *is* a big kite!" said Aarti. "Now turn that way," said Usha. All three girls scooched around.

"It *is* a big dipper!" said Gloria.

They scooched again.

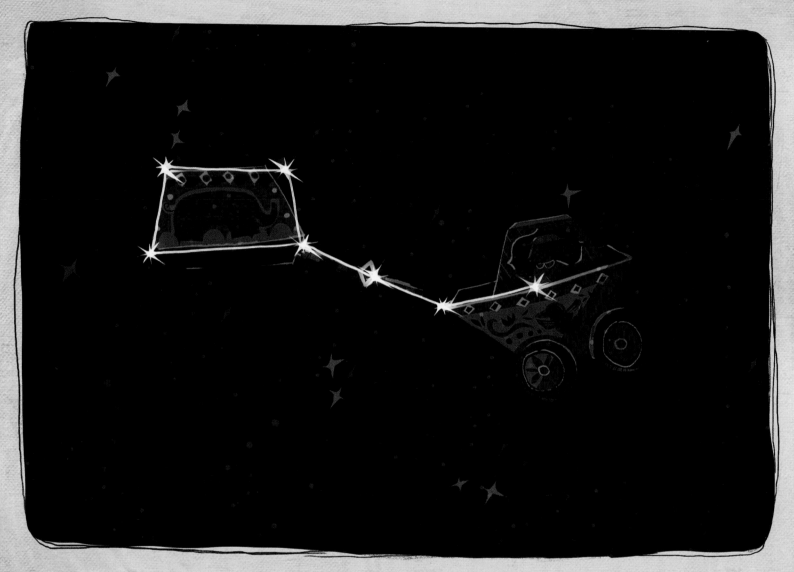

Aarti and Gloria gasped.
"And there's . . .

THE BIG DIGGER."

"What about that one?" Usha asked.

Aarti gave Usha a squeeze. "It's you, Usha!"

"Guess what you're doing," said Gloria.

"What?" asked Usha.

Seeing Stories in the Stars

Strictly speaking, the Big Dipper isn't a constellation. It's an asterism, or a recognizable group of stars. This asterism is part of the constellation Ursa Major, or the Great Bear as named by ancient Greeks. Today in the United States, we connect seven of Ursa Major's stars into a dipper, or ladle. According to folklore, African people who were enslaved in the southern United States saw a drinking gourd in these same stars and used it to navigate north to freedom. The Anishinaabe people, who live in the Great Lakes region, see it as a fisher (a furry creature related to weasels).

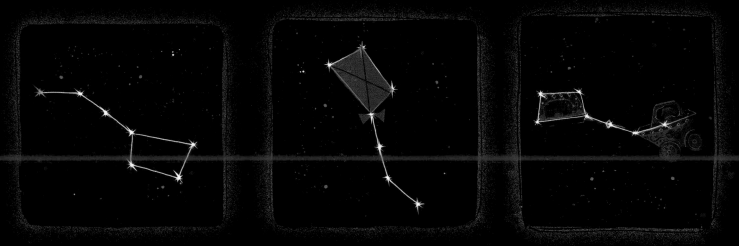

Tip: A star wheel or phone app can help you find constellations.

Around the world, different cultures see different pictures in the same stars. In Europe, people see the Big Dipper as a wagon, saucepan, or plow. In North Africa, the Tuareg people see it as a camel. In India, where my parents are from, the seven stars are called the Saptarishi, or Seven Sages. One of the stars in the group is actually a double star—two stars that look close together from Earth. These stars are said to be the sage Vasishtha and his wife, Arundhati.

While writing this book, I had fun finding silly pictures in the Big Dipper and imagining stories about them. What do you see in the stars?

—Amitha Jagannath Knight

Exploring the Math

While staring up at the same seven stars, Aarti, Usha, and Gloria each see something different. Aarti sees the Big Dipper, Usha sees the Big Digger, and Gloria sees the Big Kite. Usha eventually figures out that they see different things because they are looking at the sky from different orientations.

As the girls turn and change positions, they explore rotation, orientation, perspective, and other geometric and spatial concepts. Young children with strong spatial skills can do better in math and science in school.

Try This!

- **One person uses blocks or boxes to build something;** the others try to copy it. For an extra challenge, give children just a minute to look at the original before trying to create a replica from memory.

- **With your children, take photos of an object from different angles and perspectives.** Talk about how and why the pictures vary.

- **One person secretly picks an object in the room and describes what it would look like upside down.** The others try to identify it.

- **Talk about positions and orientations during everyday interactions.** "The tree is to the left of the house." "Let's turn this book around so we can see the spine."

As you go about the day with children, look for opportunities to point out how orientation and point of view can affect what we see. What's right side up looks upside down when you stand on your head!

— Geetha Ramani, PhD
Associate Professor, Department of Human Development and Quantitative Methodology, University of Maryland

Visit www.charlesbridge.com/storytellingmath for more activities.

To my daughters and nieces,
and to the real Usha—A. J. K.

To my teachers—S. P.

This book is supported in part by TERC under a grant
from the Heising-Simons Foundation.

At the time of publication, all URLs printed in this
book were accurate and active. Charlesbridge, TERC,
the author, and the illustrator are not responsible for
the content or accessibility of any website.

Developed in conjunction with TERC
2067 Massachusetts Avenue
Cambridge, MA 02140
(617) 873-9600
www.terc.edu

Published by Charlesbridge
9 Galen Street
Watertown, MA 02472
(617) 926-0329
www.charlesbridge.com

Printed in China
(hc) 10 9 8 7 6 5 4 3 2 1
(pb) 10 9 8 7 6 5 4 3 2 1

Library of Congress Cataloging-in-Publication Data
Names: Knight, Amitha Jagannath, author. | Prabhat, Sandhya,
    illustrator.
Title: Usha and the Big Digger / by Amitha Jagannath Knight;
    illustrated by Sandhya Prabhat.
Description: Watertown, MA: Charlesbridge Publishing, [2021]
    | Series: Storytelling math | Audience: Ages 3–6. | Audience:
    Grades K–1. | Summary: "Sisters Usha and Aarti and cousin
    Gloria see different things in the stars—a Big Dipper, a Big
    Digger, and a Big Kite—in this introduction to geometry and
    spatial relationships."—Provided by publisher.
Identifiers: LCCN 2020017261 (print) | LCCN 2020017262 (ebook)
    | ISBN 9781623542023 (hardcover) | ISBN 9781623542016
    (trade paperback) | ISBN 9781632899538 (ebook)
Subjects: CYAC: Constellations—Fiction. | Geometry—Fiction. |
    Space perception—Fiction. | East Indian Americans—Fiction.
Classification: LCC PZ7.1.K659 Us 2021 (print) | LCC PZ7.1.K659
    (ebook) | DDC [E]—dc23
LC record available at https://lccn.loc.gov/2020017261
LC ebook record available at https://lccn.loc.gov/2020017262

Illustrations done in digital media
Display type set in Canvas Text by Yellow Design Studio
Text type set in Mikado by Hannes von Döhren
Color separations and printing by 1010 Printing International
    Limited in Huizhou, Guangdong, China
Production supervision by Jennifer Most Delaney
Designed by Jon Simeon